THE URBANA FREE LIBRARY

3 1 00957 2567

W9-AHQ-909

Bear about Town
Ours en ville

Stella Blackstone
Debbie Harter

The Urbana Free Library
To renew: call 217-367-4057
or go to urbanafreelibrary.org
and select My Account

DISCARDED BY THE
URBANA FREE LIBRARY

Barefoot Books
step inside a story

HONEY HOUSE
LA MAISON DU MIEL

Bear goes to town
every day.

Ours va en ville
tous les jours.

He likes to walk
all the way.

Il aime marcher
pour y aller.

**On Mondays,
he goes to the bakery.**

BOULANGERIE

Lundi,
il s'arrête à la boulangerie.

**On Tuesdays,
he goes for a swim.**

Mardi,
il va nager.

On Wednesdays, he watches a film.

Mercredi,
il regarde un film.

**On Thursdays,
he visits the gym.**

Jeudi,
il fait de la gym.

**On Fridays,
he goes to the toyshop.**

Vendredi,
il visite le magasin de jouets.

On Saturdays,
he strolls through the park.

Samedi,
il se promène dans le parc.

On Sundays, he goes to the playground,

Dimanche,
il se rend à l'aire de jeux,

And plays with his friends until dark.

Et s'amuse avec ses amis
jusqu'à la tombée de la nuit.

Find the places
Bear visits each day.

Retrouve les lieux qu'Ours
fréquente chaque jour.

Vocabulary /
Vocabulaire

Monday – lundi
Tuesday – mardi
Wednesday – mercredi
Thursday – jeudi
Friday – vendredi
Saturday – samedi
Sunday – dimanche

Barefoot Books
2067 Massachusetts Ave
Cambridge, MA 02140

Barefoot Books
29/30 Fitzroy Square
London, W1T 6LQ

Text copyright © 2000 by Stella Blackstone
Illustration copyright © 2000 by Debbie Harter
The moral rights of Stella Blackstone and Debbie Harter have been asserted

First published in the United States of America by Barefoot Books, Inc
and in Great Britain by Barefoot Books, Ltd in 2000
This bilingual French edition first published in 2017
All rights reserved

Translation by Jennifer Couëlle
Reproduction by Bright Arts, Hong Kong
Printed in China on 100% acid-free paper
This book was typeset in Futura and Slappy
The illustrations were prepared in watercolor, pen and ink, and crayon

ISBN 978-1-78285-329-9

British Cataloguing-in-Publication Data: a catalogue record for this book is available from the British Library

Library of Congress Cataloging-in-Publication Data is available upon request

3 5 7 9 8 6 4 2